THE Disney COLLECTION

PIANO · VOCAL · GUITAR

W9-DAQ-865

Hal Leonard Publishing Corporation

41814

ISBN 0-88188-854-0
All art © 1988 The Walt Disney Music Company

THE
DISNEY
COLLECTION

Best-Loved Songs from Disney Motion Pictures, Television, and Theme Parks

He introduced dozens of classic songs to the world, and yet he never had any training as a songwriter. He was one of the great musical innovators of our time, but he couldn't play an instrument.

His name was Walt Disney, and music was as much a part of his work as the colorful animation which made him famous. He achieved such a complete synthesis of sight and sound that composer Jerome Kern said: "Cartoonist Walt Disney has made the twentieth century's only important contribution to music. Disney has made use of music as language. In the synchronization of humorous episodes with humorous music, he has unquestionably given us the outstanding contribution of our time."

Disney began developing his ideas about music early in his animation career. After all, Mickey Mouse made his screen debut in the first fully synchronized sound cartoon, *Steamboat Willie* (1928). Out of Mickey's success came the Silly Symphonies, a series of cartoons built entirely around music. Such shorts as *Flowers and Trees* (1932), *Lullaby Land* (1933), and *The Flying Mouse* (1934) are vivid examples of how Disney used music and song not only to establish mood, but more importantly to tell the story and achieve personality.

During production of his first animated feature, *Snow White and the Seven Dwarfs* (1937), Disney began concretely defining his approach to song as story. "It can still be good music and not follow the same pattern everybody in the country has followed," Disney said of the Snow White songs. "Really we should set a new pattern—a new way to use music—weave it into the story so somebody doesn't just burst into song." Thus, years before Broadway or Hollywood integrated music and narrative, Disney was pioneering a tuneful new way of telling a story.

Disney had the showman's instinct for what the public likes. "If he felt a song was enjoyable for him," said Richard Sherman of the Sherman brothers songwriting team, "then he felt ninety percent of the people that saw the picture would enjoy that same song." Disney's judgement has been borne out by the fact that so many of his films contained that rarest of musical wonders, the hit song that endures.

The national music charts, however, were of secondary concern to Disney. "We wanted the songs to stand on their own merits," he admitted, "and most of them did very well. But our first concern was to make sure that each song helped us tell our story."

Disney worked with the most creative of musical talents and he knew it. "Credit for the memorable songs and scores must, of course, go to the brilliant composers and musicians who have been associated with me through the years." It was these composers who set Disney's ideas to music, who defined every Disney project in song—including not just motion pictures, but television programs and theme park rides.

"Walt understood that a song is what people carry away with them," songwriter Robert Sherman has said. "People can go to a Disney picture or park and be enchanted by it, but when they go home, the song is what they keep."

ZIP-A-DEE-DOO-DAH

"I was familiar with the Uncle Remus tales since boyhood,"said Walt Disney. "From the time I began making animation features, I have had them definitely in my production plans." Disney brought the famed folk tales of Joel Chandler Harris to animated life in *Song of the South*, featuring Brer Rabbit and the other critters of the Uncle Remus stories. Disney's celebrated love for new words and phrases was evident in the film's central song, "Zip-A-Dee-Doo-Dah," a word Walt is said to have coined. Sung by James Baskett as Uncle Remus, the song provided a link between live-action reality and the cartoon fantasy world of Brer Rabbit. "Zip-A-Dee-Doo-Dah," honored with an Academy Award as Best Song, expresses the optimism at the heart of Uncle Remus's wise and warm fables.

WHISTLE WHILE YOU WORK

"Of all the characters in the fairy tales," Walt Disney remembered, "I loved *Snow White* best, and when I planned my first full-length cartoon, she inevitably was the heroine." *Snow White and the Seven Dwarfs* is Walt Disney's personal masterpiece. "I don't think any other picture ever had as much of Walt in it, in terms of creativity," contended animator Woolie Reitherman. "Even the songs were generated by his creativity." From the earliest planning stages, Disney envisioned his first animated feature as a musical. Frank Churchill and Larry Morey wrote twenty-five tunes in search of the "perfect" songs. Of the eight songs Disney used in the film, six were hits and have become, like the film itself, a permanent part of our culture.

When Disney first began developing *Snow White*, he called the project his "Feature Symphony," a reference to the Silly Symphony cartoons that served as a proving ground for Walt's style of musical story-telling. "Whistle While You Work" is the bouncy basis for the extended sequence most reminiscent of the Silly Symphonies. Snow White cheerfully sings and whistles the song as she and her animal friends clean up the dwarfs' cottage. The song is performed by Adriana Caselotti as the voice of Snow White.

CHIM CHIM CHER-EE

Widely acclaimed as Walt Disney's greatest film achievement, *Mary Poppins* is also considered one of Hollywood's best musical films. Disney signed top talent to bring the original P.L. Travers stories to tuneful life. Prolific Disney tunesmiths Richard and Robert Sherman were assigned to write the songs, while Irwin Kostal was recruited from Broadway to supervise, arrange, and conduct the music. Julie Andrews was the toast of Broadway, but she became an internationally renowned movie star with her Oscar-winning motion picture debut as Mary Poppins. Dick Van Dyke, then at the peak of his popularity as a television performer, was cast as jack-of-all-trades Bert. Walt Disney combined all these elements and more into pure movie magic, and *Mary Poppins* became the most popular of the showman's films.

A story sketch of a chimney sweep by *Mary Poppins'* co-writer Don DaGradi inspired the Shermans to compose "Chim Chim Cher-ee." Said Robert Sherman, "One look and we knew this was music, this had to be a song." The result became the heart of the picture's chimney sweep sequence, capturing both the plucky spirit of the sweeps and the haunting beauty of the rooftop world that only they see. "Chim Chim Cher-ee" was awarded an Oscar as Best Song, and the Sherman brothers' score won the Academy Award for Best Original Score.

THE BARE NECESSITIES

The Jungle Book, a freewheeling adaptation of the Rudyard Kipling stories, featured "name" voices that had a strong influence on the personalities of the cartoon charcters. The animators had trouble developing the happy-go-lucky bear, Baloo, until Walt Disney suggested gravel-voiced Phil Harris for the role. Harris's breezy bandleader lingo turned Baloo from a supporting player into the film's musical star.

Written by Terry Gilkyson, "The Bare Necessities" expresses Baloo's carefree attitude toward life. The song's cool Dixieland-like jungle harmonies are performed in Phil Harris's with-the-beat style. "Working for Walt Disney," commented Harris, "I mean, it's not like working at all. I just play myself." Harris later said that playing Baloo has made him immortal, winning him new fans each time the movie is seen. Nominated for a Best Song Academy Award, "The Bare Necessities" has joined the long list of Disney standards.

ONCE UPON A DREAM

Walt Disney had long admired Tchaikovsky's expressive *Sleeping Beauty Ballet*, and he felt the music was essential to his animated version of the fairy tale. George Bruns, one of the studio's top composers and most accomplished musicians, adapted the classic work for the film's romantic songs and orchestrations. "About one-third of the original ballet was preserved," said Bruns, "and even in the adaptation the original flavor was never lost." Bruns traveled to Germany to record the music, played by the Berlin Symphony Orchestra with state-of-the-art, six-channel stereo equipment.

Versatile songwriters Sammy Fain and Jack Lawrence adapted "Once Upon a Dream"the one *Sleeping Beauty* song not by George Bruns—from the Tchaikovsky ballet. Mary Costa is the voice of Princess Aurora, a role she auditioned for while still in high school. She has since achieved fame in the world of opera, making numerous appearances at the Metropolitan Opera in New York City. "But *Sleeping Beauty* is the thing I'm most proud of in my entire career," she has said. "It's a beautiful film to be associated with and I was thrilled to be able to do it."

I'VE GOT NO STRINGS

Having established the animated feature as an art form with *Snow White,* Walt Disney set out to top himself with *Pinocchio.* Disney embellished the film with time-consuming detail, and the Oscar-winning score complements the film's lavish visuals. Distinguished author/illustrator Maurice Sendak wrote in 1978 that "the most significant feature, for me, is the musical score. A number of reviews compared the songs unfavorably to the more tuneful *Snow White* music. What they failed to realize is that the score is a vital, integral part of the whole; nothing was allowed to obtrude even at the risk of sacrificing obvious melody and the hit song charts."

Composer Leigh Harline sat in on the story conference and voice recording sessions, making certain that story points and characters were established with his melodies. Today, *Pinocchio* is widely considered the most magnificent animated feature ever made, its enduring charm enhanced by the enchanting music.

Pinocchio himself sings the jaunty tune "I've Got No Strings," stopping the show in Stromboli's puppet theatre. This is the little woodenhead's one big song, charmingly performed by child actor Dickie Jones. The song is staged as an elaborate production number, starring the amateurish but stagestruck Pinocchio, who is surrounded by a bewildering succession of marionette co-stars and ever-changing backdrops.

YOU CAN FLY! YOU CAN FLY! YOU CAN FLY!

"Next to Snow White, I cared most for Peter Pan," Walt Disney once revealed. "When I began producing cartoons, *Peter Pan* was high on my list of subjects." Disney released his animated version of Sir James Barrie's classic in 1953. The songs are skillfully integrated into the screen story; as film scholar Leonard Maltin has pointed out in *The Disney Films,* "the songs are introduced, and sometimes sung in fragments, or so naturally that one is hardly aware that they have begun." Disney signed experienced composers Sammy Cahn and Sammy Fain to write songs, with other tunes contributed by Disney veterans such as Oliver Wallace, Ted Sears, and Frank Churchill..

"You Can Fly! You Can Fly! You Can Fly!" is introduced by Peter Pan with Wendy, John, and Michael Darling, speaking the lyrics rhythmically but naturally,

before the chorus takes up the song as the children fly off for Never Land. Disney live-action star Bobby Driscoll was the voice and model for Peter Pan, and Kathryn Beaumont, the voice of *Alice in Wonderland* (1951), spoke as Wendy.

WHO'S AFRAID OF THE BIG BAD WOLF?

Begun in 1929 as an artistic proving ground for the Disney animators, the Silly Symphony series emphasized musical themes. At first, classical music or popular songs in the public domain were the main ingredient, but for *Three Little Pigs* Walt Disney felt a new song should be written to tie all the elements together. In adapting the old fable, Disney had already decided the pigs should have musical instruments. Fifer Pig and Fiddler Pig played their namesake instruments with carefree abandon, while Practical Pig performed on his very practical brick piano.

In writing "Who's Afraid of the Big Bad Wolf?," Disney composer Frank Churchill—former honky-tonk pianist and radio and movie studio musician—came up with a simple yet catchy jingle. Storyman Ted Sears threw in a few couplets (additional lyrics were written by Ann Ronell), and when there seemed to be no way to end the chorus, studio musician/voiceman Pinto Colvig suggested simply finishing with a few bars of the fiddle or fife.

Three Little Pigs was a smash hit, and "Who's Afraid of the Big Bad Wolf?" became the rallying cry of a Depression-weary nation. "*Three Little Pigs* came out at just the right psychological moment," Walt Disney later observed. "In 1933, a lot of people were talking about keeping the wolf from the door. At any rate, both the picture and the song were important to us in another way. They showed us the value of telling a story through a song." Honored with an Academy Award as Best Short Subject, this cartoon paved the way for Disney's feature films, and "Who's Afraid of the Big Bad Wolf?"—the first Disney song hit and certainly the first hit ever to come from an animated cartoon—helped *Three Little Pigs* become the most popular cartoon short of all time.

LOVE IS A SONG

Bambi is the gently told tale of a deer coming of age in the forest. The animated feature's musical score, nominated for an Academy Award, reflects nature's drama as it unfolds in the lives of Bambi, Thumper the rabbit, and Flower the skunk. Major production numbers are passed over in favor of songs sung offscreen by a forty-voice choir, enhancing the film's delicate atmosphere.

Bambi opens with "Love Is a Song," setting a poetic tone that perfectly fits the loveliest of Disney's animated features. The tune is used both in the song itself and as a motif recurring throughout. As the cycle of nature repeats itself with the birth of Bambi's children, so the film comes full circle to conclude with "Love Is a Song," nominated for an Academy Award as Best Song..

CASEY JR.

Dumbo, the story of the little elephant whose enormous ears enable him to fly, was acclaimed as Walt Disney's most endearing, least pretentious animated feature. The circus is the background for *Dumbo*, and the rousing songs capture the atmosphere of tents, clowns, and thrilling animal acts. "Casey Jr." musically conveys all the color and excitement of the Big Top returning to town via the comical little circus train "coming down the track." *Dumbo's* music won the Academy Award as Best Score of 1941.

THE WORK SONG

For *Cinderella*, his first single-story full-length animated feature after World War II, Walt Disney signed the songwriting team of Mack David, Al Hoffman, and Jerry Livingston. In New York's Tin Pan Alley, they had conjured up a catchy novelty tune, "Chi-Baba, Chi-Baba," which seemed to suggest to Disney the magical quality he wanted.

"Walt had in mind some type of ballet sound for 'The Work Song,'" songwriter Jerry Livingston remembered. "But after we looked at the storyboards and discussed the action of the animals scurrying about, we knew we needed something light, yet frantic." The resulting song comically demonstrates the loyalty of the birds and mice as they make a beautiful gown so their beloved "Cinderelly" can attend the Royal Ball.

Because of "The Work Song" and its other hit tunes, *Cinderella's* musical score was nominated for an Academy Award.

THE SECOND STAR TO THE RIGHT

"The Second Star to the Right" is the evocative, lullaby-like opening to *Peter Pan*. Wistfully sung over the main titles by a chorus, the song conveys the nostalgic allure of Never Land and sets the stage for the fantasy about to unfold. Composer Sammy Fain commented that "Walt impressed me with his uncanny ear for what type of music would work in his pictures."

HI-DIDDLE-DEE-DEE

Each of *Pinocchio's* songs skillfully illustrates a mood, characterization, or plot development. "Hi-Diddle-Dee-Dee," sung by character actor Walter Catlett as the scheming fox J. Worthington ("Honest John") Foulfellow, seems to celebrate the glories of theatrical stardom. The song is deceptive in its high spirits, however, for the crafty fox uses it to lure the innocent Pinocchio from the straight-and-narrow onto the wicked, wicked stage.

EV'RYBODY WANTS TO BE A CAT

The Aristocats portrays a quartet of high-society cats with a back-alley "swinger" in 1910 Paris. This animated feature—the first produced by the studio after Walt Disney's death—tells its story with carefree comedy and jazzy music. "Ev'rybody Wants to Be a Cat" especially demonstrates the jazz influence. Composer George Bruns, who scored the film, points out that "the jazz theme underscores the jam session in the second half of the picture and also the O'Malley and Scat Cat characters." These two "hep cats" are voiced by Phil Harris and Scatman Crothers, who have a field day scattin' and singin'.

ONE SONG

In producing *Snow White and the Seven Dwarfs*, Walt Disney and his staff struggled with the challenge of animating believable human figures. Finally, after much experimentation, inspiration, and just plain hard work, a graceful, charming Snow White was achieved. The animators had more trouble with the Prince; consequently, he is onscreen for only a brief time. He makes a good first impression on Snow White and the audience, however, with the ballad "One Song," performed by Harry Stockwell. The Prince sings of "one love, only for you" as Snow White shyly listens from the palace balcony. It is the character's only moment in the spotlight until the end of the film, when he awakens Snow White with love's first kiss.

WINNIE THE POOH

Walt Disney's animated tale about the "silly old bear" and his quest for honey preserves the gentle whimsy of the original stories by A.A. Milne. For songwriters Richard and Robert Sherman, however, the particular feel of the Winnie the Pooh stories was at first elusive.

"When Walt asked us to read *Winnie-the-Pooh*," recalls Richard Sherman, "we couldn't get with the subject right away. One day during the filming of *Mary Poppins*, we asked Julie Andrews's then-husband, Tony Walton, about Pooh, since he was raised in England. He spent several hours with us explaining how important the Pooh stories were to him while he was growing up. He identified with pudgy Pooh, who always came out on top. We finally had a feeling of how to understand the stories, how to get to the heart of them." The Shermans' theme song for Pooh perfectly captures the charm of Milne's "enchanted neighborhood."

CRUELLA DE VILLE

101 Dalmations was a departure for the Disney Studio not only in animation style but in musical storytelling. Unlike previous tune-filled features, *101 Dalmations* has only three songs. Ironically, the lead human, Roger Radcliff, is a songwriter! Roger composes a blues number paying homage to the flamboyant craftiness of the meddlesome madwoman, Cruella De Ville. He then takes mischievous delight in singing this song when Cruella comes to call, providing one of the musical highlights of *101 Dalmations*.

SO THIS IS LOVE

"So This Is Love," sung in Cinderella's thoughts as she dances with the Prince at the Royal Ball, musically conveys her dreams of romance. Cinderella's expressive voice is that of Ilene Woods, a singer on radio's *Hit Parade*, who was cast by Walt Disney after she auditioned one of the film's songs as a favor to the composers.

THE SIAMESE CAT SONG

Sultry song-stylist Peggy Lee was at the top of the charts when Walt Disney chose her as the voice of Lady in *Lady and the Tramp*. But as she got involved with story conferences, she discovered the film's musical possibilities. Before long, Disney cast Barbara Luddy as Lady and signed Peggy Lee and composer Sonny Burke to pen the picture's five songs. Lee provides several voices in the final picture, and her vocal versatility is matched by her varied songs, which

gracefully complement *Lady and the Tramp*'s elegant animation.

In "The Siamese Cat Song," the sneakiness of the intruding Siamese cats, Si and Am, is stated through the clever music and lyrics. In this song Peggy Lee sings a duet with herself, capturing the cats' exotic flair for mischief.

SOMEONE'S WAITING FOR YOU

Secret-agent mice Bernard and Miss Bianca are the lead characters in *The Rescuers*, but the plight of Penny the orphan girl is at the heart of the film. The Academy-Award-nominated song "Someone's Waiting for You" reflects Penny's tender hope that there's someone somewhere who will love her. The ballad was written by legendary tunesmith Sammy Fain, with words by Carol Connors and Ayn Robbins, the team responsible for the lyrics of the original *Rocky* theme.

IT'S A SMALL WORLD

"One day," remembered songwriter Richard Sherman, "Walt took my brother and me to where they developed special projects for Walt. He explained that they were building a World's Fair exhibit for UNICEF. The idea was to show the universality of man. Walt took us through a mock-up with mechanical dolls in native costumes from around the world, each singing their respective national songs." It was over this cacophony of sound that Disney told the Shermans what he wanted: "a song that is universal, that can be sung in any language, with any type of instrumentation, simultaneously." The brothers met the challenge, composing a simple but bright two-part song that could be sung as a round or in counterpoint. One of the most widely known of the Disney songs, "It's a Small World" is heard by thousands every day at the Disney theme parks.

BABY MINE

"Baby Mine" provides a poignant contrast to *Dumbo's* boisterous circus background. The tender lullaby is sung by an offscreen chorus, while the imprisoned Mrs. Jumbo cradles her tearful Dumbo, and the other circus animals and their babies settle down for the night. "Baby Mine" was an Academy Award nominee as Best Song.

THE MICKEY MOUSE CLUB MARCH

Every weekday afternoon from 1955 through 1959, millions of youngsters eagerly gathered around their television sets to watch *The Mickey Mouse Club*. Few children's shows have ever rivaled the popularity and impact of this phenomenally successful program. A talented group of youngsters ("Annette!" "Lonnie!" "Darlene!") sang and danced up a storm between the cartoons, newsreels, and serials.

Scores of original songs were performed on the show, many of them written by chief Mouseketeer Jimmie Dodd. In planning the program, Walt Disney had called for a "club song," and Dodd came up with "The Mickey Mouse Club March," featuring the famous "M-I-C-K-E-Y M-O-U-S-E" chant.

THE MICKEY MOUSE CLUB ALMA MATER

At the end of each *Mickey Mouse Club* episode, the Mouseketeers bid us farewell with a heartfelt "Alma Mater" version of the march. "See you real soon...Why? Because we *like* you!"

WHEN YOU WISH UPON A STAR

Having established the full-length animated feature as an art form with *Snow White*, Walt Disney set out to top himself with *Pinocchio*. Disney embellished the film with time-consuming detail, and the Oscar-winning score complements the film's lavish visuals. Distinguished author and illustrator Maurice Sendak wrote in 1978 that "the most significant feature, for me, is the musical score. A number of reviews compared the songs unfavorably to the more tuneful *Snow White* music. What they failed to realize is that the score is a vital, integral part of the whole; nothing was allowed to obtrude even at the risk of sacrificing obvious melody and the hit song charts."

Composer Leigh Harline sat in on the story conferences and voice recording sessions, making certain that story points and characters were established with his melodies. Today, *Pinocchio* is widely considered the most magnificent animated feature ever made, its enduring charm enhanced by the enchanting music. *Pinocchio's* "conscience," Jiminy Cricket, was at first an elusive personality for Disney and his animators, but with thoughtful character design and the sprightly voice of Cliff "Ukulele Ike" Edwards, the cricket emerged as a new Disney star. Jiminy opens *Pinocchio* by crooning the lyrical ballad "When You Wish Upon a Star." Disney animators Frank Thomas and Ollie Johnston observed, "A song that catches the exact mood of a film's sequence and expresses it in a fresh and memorable way will do wonders for the film, and for the composer, too. Leigh Harline and Ned Washington's lovely 'When You Wish Upon a Star' served double duty, introducing us to a cricket with a gentle personality as well as setting a mood for the whole picture to follow."

The song was the first from a Disney film to be awarded the Academy Award as Best Song, and it was an instant popular hit, smashing national music chart records. It's been recorded by such diverse artists as Glenn Miller, Chet Atkins, the rock group Kiss and, most recently, Linda Ronstadt. It is Jiminy Cricket's original version, however, that remains everyone's favorite.

S UPERCALIFRAGILISTICEXPIALIDO-CIOUS Widely acclaimed as Walt Disney's greatest film achievement, *Mary Poppins* is also considered one of Hollywood's best musical films. Disney signed top talent to bring the original P.L. Travers stories to tuneful life. Prolific Disney tunesmiths Richard and Robert Sherman were assigned to write the songs, while Irwin Kostal was recruited from Broadway to supervise, arrange, and conduct the music. Julie Andrews was the toast of Broadway, but she became an internationally renowned movie star with her Oscar-winning motion picture debut as Mary Poppins. Dick Van Dyke, then at the peak of his popularity as a television performer, was cast as jack-of-all-trades Bert. Walt Disney combined all these elements and more into pure movie magic, and *Mary Poppins* became the most popular of the showman's films. The Sherman brothers' score won the Academy Award for Best Original Score.

Walt Disney, never satisfied with the conventional, loved new words and phrases. Undoubtedly the most outrageous word ever created for a Disney song came from *Mary Poppins*. Coined by the Shermans, it was a kind of musical talisman intended to bring the Banks children back from the animated fantasy world into reality. "As kids," explained Richard Sherman, "my brother and I went to the Adirondacks for summer camp, and we recall that one summer we had learned a word similar to 'Supercalifragilisticexpialidocious.' It gave us kids a word that no adult had. It was our own special word, and we wanted the Banks children to have the same feeling."

H E'S A TRAMP
Sultry song-stylist Peggy Lee was at the top of the charts when Walt Disney chose her as the voice of Lady in *Lady and the Tramp*. But as she got involved with story conferences, she discovered the film's musical possibilities. Before long, Disney cast Barbara Luddy as Lady and signed Peggy Lee and composer Sonny Burke to pen the picture's five songs. Lee provides several voices in the final picture, and her vocal versatility is matched by her varied songs, which gracefully complement *Lady and the Tramp's* elegant animation.

In recording "He's a Tramp," Peggy Lee gave animator Eric Larson a model for the seductive on-screen movements of Peg, the faded Pekingese showgirl. Lee's sassy vocals and Larson's vampish animation of Peg combined to make "He's a Tramp" the equivalent of a Broadway show-stopper. The Mello Men vocal group provides a raucous background of yips and howls as Peg opens the innocent Lady's eyes to Tramp's "past."

H EIGH-HO
(THE DWARFS' MARCHING SONG)
"Of all the characters in the fairy tales," Walt Disney remembered, "I loved Snow White best, and when I planned my first full-length cartoon, she inevitably was the heroine."

Snow White and the Seven Dwarfs is Walt Disney's personal masterpiece. "I don't think any other picture ever had as much of Walt in it, in terms of creativity," contended animator Woolie Reitherman. "Even the songs were generated by his creativity." From the earliest planning stages, Disney envisioned his first animated feature as a musical. Frank Churchill and Larry Morey wrote twenty-five tunes in search of the "perfect" songs. Of the eight songs Disney used in the film, six were hits and have become, like the film itself, a permanent part of our culture.

Disney sensed that the lovable, comical dwarfs were the key to the story, and he was determined to give seven distinctly different personalities to these formerly shadowy figures. In addition, they needed a theme song that would endear them to the audience. The answer was "Heigh-Ho," a simple but catchy tune sung by the dwarfs as they "dig,dig,dig" in their diamond mine and then march home through the woods.

A DREAM IS A WISH YOUR HEART MAKES

For *Cinderella*, his first single-story full-length animated feature after World War II, Walt Disney signed the songwriting team of Mack David, Al Hoffman, and Jerry Livingston. In New York's Tin Pan Alley they had conjured up a catchy novelty tune, "Chi-Baba, Chi-Baba," which seemed to suggest to Disney the magical quality he wanted. His judgment was borne out, as *Cinderella's* score was nominated for an Academy Award.

In "A Dream Is a Wish Your Heart Makes," radio singing star Ilene Woods enchantingly vocalizes for Cinderella, a role given to her by Walt Disney after he heard her audition one of the film's songs as a favor to the composers.

L ITTLE APRIL SHOWER

Bambi is the gently told tale of a deer coming of age in the forest. The animated feature's musical score, nominated for an Academy Award, reflects nature's drama as it unfolds in the lives of Bambi, Thumper the rabbit, and Flower the skunk. Major production numbers are passed over in favor of songs sung offscreen by a forty-voice choir, enhancing the film's delicate atmosphere.

"Little April Shower" is the musical background for one of the most striking sequences in Bambi. The rhythm of the rain was keyed and animated to Frank Churchill's music, and Larry Morey's lyrics were sung in such a way as to suggest falling raindrops.

W HEN I SEE AN ELEPHANT FLY

Dumbo, the story of the little elephant whose enormous ears enable him to fly, was acclaimed as Walt Disney's most endearing, least pretentious animated feature. Disney storyman Dick Huemer, who adapted *Dumbo* for the screen with Joe Grant, reported that lyricist Ned Washington "would be in on story meetings and would present his songs. He'd tap them out with his fingers." *Dumbo's* music won the Academy Award as Best Score of 1941.

"When I See an Elephant Fly" is the pun-filled song in which the sarcastic crows taunt Dumbo when Timothy Mouse suspects the baby elephant can fly. "The situation of the crows picking on little Dumbo was sound story construction," said Dick Huemer. "Either dialog or song would bring it off, but a song would be...a much more entertaining way than just saying, 'Look who's trying to fly!' In a song you can bring out all these points painlessly, delightfully."

S OME DAY MY PRINCE WILL COME

During the development of *Snow White*, Walt Disney felt that the love of the young Princess for the Prince was a key ingredient in the story. He encouraged Morey and Churchill to write a song expressing that love, and the result was "Some Day My Prince Will Come," Snow White's tuneful telling of her favorite dream to her newfound friends, the seven dwarfs. Adriana Caselotti, the voice of Snow White, recalled that "all the dialog and musical portions were done in a few days, but I felt very blessed. Not everyone gets to introduce a song like 'Some Day My Prince Will Come.'"

A SPOONFUL OF SUGAR

In writing the music for *Mary Poppins*, the Sherman brothers spoke to Julie Andrews about developing a "keynote" song for Mary Poppins herself. "(Julie) felt that Mary Poppins wouldn't say things directly," remembers Robert Sherman. "So we dug and dug and dug and then one day my son came home from school. He said he'd been given a vaccination not with a needle but with the medicine on a lump of sugar. And the next day, I said to Dick, 'A spoonful of sugar helps the medicine go down.'" The result: Mary Poppins had a directly indirect way of expressing herself with "A Spoonful of Sugar."

B IBBIDI-BOBBIDI-BOO

In adapting *Cinderella* for animation, Disney characterized the Fairy God-mother as a kindly, tittering woman, "not goofy or stupid but rather as having a wonderful sense of humor...We can get personality into the song," concluded Disney. The Oscar-nominated "Bibbidi-Bobbidi-Boo" succeeds in doing just that. It embodies the jovial, magical godmother, voiced by Disney favorite Verna Felton. Both "Bibbidi-Bobbidi-Boo" and "A Dream Is a Wish Your Heart Makes" sold over a million records, and the songs shared the top two spots on television's Hit Parade.

B ELLA NOTTE

In *Lady and the Tramp*, the romantic "Bella Notte" sets the mood for one of the most memorable scenes in Disney animation: Lady and Tramp eating spaghetti outside Tony's Italian restaurant. The two dogs fall in puppy love as Tony and his chef serenade them, accompanied by mandolins, under the "sky with stars in her eyes."

FOLLOWING THE LEADER

"Next to Snow White, I cared most for Peter Pan," Walt Disney once revealed. "When I began producing cartoons, *Peter Pan* was high on my list of subjects." Disney released his animated version of Sir James Barrie's classic in 1953. The songs are skillfully integrated into the screen story; as film scholar Leonard Maltin has pointed out in *The Disney Films*, "the songs are introduced, and sometimes sung in fragments, or so naturally that one is hardly aware that they have begun." Disney signed experienced composers Sammy Cahn and Sammy Fain to write songs, with other tunes contributed by Disney veterans such as Oliver Wallace, Ted Sears, and Frank Churchill.

In developing a theme to identify Peter's Never Land companions, the Lost Boys, Walt conferred with composer Oliver Wallace. "You know," said Disney, "these Lost Boys are just young kids marching along after the leader, sort of making up a keep-up song." Disney came up with a simple "tee dum, tee dee..." chant and Wallace played a march on the piano. "That's it!" Disney shouted, and a song, "Following the Leader," was born.

LAVENDER BLUE

"*So Dear to My Heart* was especially close to me," Walt Disney once said. "Why, that's the life my brother and I grew up with as kids out in Missouri." In the live-action/animated production, Disney captured all the warm nostalgia of a 1903 country fair and life on a farm. *So Dear to My Heart* features down-home folk songs sung by legendary balladeer Burl Ives. The film's hit song, "Lavender Blue," was nominated for an Academy Award.

THEME FROM ZORRO

The exciting exploits of the masked avenger, Zorro, were first brought to the television screen by Walt Disney in 1957. The Spanish-flavored theme, written by George Bruns and Norman Foster (writer/director of many of the *Zorro* episodes), opened each thrilling chapter in the story of Zorro. An important part of every episode—and a climactic moment in the theme itself—is the carving of the jagged "Z" by the sword of Zorro.

I WAN'NA BE LIKE YOU

The Jungle Book, a freewheeling adaptation of the Rudyard Kipling stories, featured "name" voices that had a strong influence on the personalities of the cartoon characters. The animators had trouble developing the happy-go-lucky bear, Baloo, until Walt Disney suggested gravel-voiced Phil Harris for the role. Harris's breezy bandleader lingo turned Baloo from a supporting player into the film's musical star.

As *The Jungle Book* developed, Disney felt the tone was too serious, so he called in Richard and Robert Sherman to help tell the story in a lighter, musical vein. "The first idea we came up with," recalled Richard Sherman, "was Dixieland, because we know that's fun, tap-your-toe music." The song that grew out of that meeting, "I Wan'na Be Like You," became the basis of a major sequence starring the addled ape, King Louie the Most, whose character was inspired and voiced by jazz king Louis Prima. The famous Phil Harris-Louis Prima "scat" duet was actually recorded separately. "We recorded Louis Prima first," said Richard Sherman," then several months later, Phil Harris was free to come into the studio and do his part, yet they both sound beautiful together."

I WONDER

Walt Disney had long admired Tchaikovsky's expressive *Sleeping Beauty Ballet*, and he felt the music was essential to his animated version of the fairy tale. George Bruns, one of the studio's top composers and most accomplished musicians, adapted the classic work for the film's romantic songs and orchestrations. "About one-third of the original ballet was preserved," said Bruns, "and even in the adaptation the original flavor was never lost." Bruns traveled to Germany to record the music, played by the Berlin Symphony Orchestra, with state-of-the-art six-channel stereo equipment.

"I Wonder," adapted from Tchaikovsky by Bruns with lyrics by veteran storymen Winston Hibler and Ted Sears, is wistfully sung by Princess Aurora on her fateful sixteenth birthday. Her plaintive refrain is echoed by a bluebird as, accompanied by her other woodland friends, Aurora strolls deep into the forest, longing for "someone to sing to." Opera star Mary Costa sings "I Wonder" with haunting beauty.

O-DE-LALLY

The story of "what really happened in Sherwood Forest," this animated version of the Robin Hood legend features animal characters and the laid-back music of Roger Miller. Usually labeled as a country-western performer, Miller's musical inventiveness actually has a solid basis in jazz, and his clowning lyrics reveal the sophistication of a deeply philosophical man. Miller's "Oo-De-Lally" sets the film's light-hearted tone in the opening scene, in which Robin Hood is pursued by the Sheriff of Nottingham. Roger Miller tells the musical story as Allan-a-Dale, the rooster minstrel.

BEST OF FRIENDS

Reminiscent of *Bambi* in mood and spirit, *The Fox and the Hound* tells the animated tale of two born enemies who grow up as friends. Pearl Bailey lends her warm personality and winning vocal style to the role of Big Mama, the wise owl who observes all that occurs around her. Her song, "Best of Friends," subtly brings up the conflict at the heart of the fox and hound's friendship.

YO HO (A PIRATE'S LIFE FOR ME)

In the late 1950s, Walt Disney conceived the idea of a pirate adventure, and in 1967 the Pirates of the Caribbean attraction first welcomed Disneyland guests into the thick of the action. The success of "It's a Small World" inspired Disney "Imagineers" to establish the ride's roguish atmosphere through a never-ending song. Capturing the bloodthirsty but fun-loving nature of the salty crew as they plunder the Spanish Main in the 1700's, "Yo Ho (A Pirate's Life for Me)" is one song no visitor to the Disney theme parks can forget.

WITH A SMILE AND A SONG

Pacing was an important aspect of any Walt Disney feature, and *Snow White* is one of the best examples. Disney and his crew constructed the story so that scenes follow each other in emotional as well as chronological order. After Snow White's nightmarish flight into the woods, for example, she is befriended by the lovable woodland animals. Relieved after her ordeal, Snow White sings the sunny "With a Smile and a Song."

SALUDOS AMIGOS

As war engulfed the globe in the early 1940s, the United States established a Good Neighbor policy in order to strengthen ties with her south-of-the-border neighbors. As part of that effort, the State Department asked Walt Disney to go on a goodwill tour of South America as a kind of cultural ambassador. Disney agreed to a "working tour" during which he would gather material for animated pictures about the Latin countries. So in 1941, Walt Disney and a handpicked group of artists, writers, and musicians visited Brazil, Argentina, and Chile.

Among Disney's companions was musical director Charles Wolcott. "Up until that time, my only exposure to Latin music was the sound of Xavier Cugat," recalled Wolcott. "The tour was a revealing experience, as we had the opportunity to explore the countryside and gain insight into the music of the people." Wolcott and lyricist Ned Washington summed up the good feelings generated by the Disney tour in "Saludos Amigos," the title tune of the 1943 feature developed from the South American journey. The song's cheerful expression of goodwill among neighboring nations made "Saludos Amigos" (or, in English, "Hello, Friends") popular on both sides of the border and earned an Academy Award nomination as Best Song. "While half of this world is being forced to shout 'Heil Hitler,'" said Walt Disney, "our answer is to say, 'Saludos Amigos.'"

THE BALLAD OF DAVY CROCKETT

For his new *Disneyland* anthology television series, Walt Disney decided to tell the story of frontiersman Davy Crockett. Disney felt that a musical element was needed to bridge the gaps between adventures, so he asked George Bruns to compose a "little throwaway melody." Bruns went to *Crockett* screenwriter Tom Blackburn for lyrics, and a half hour later the pair returned with a song that became "The Ballad of Davy Crockett." When the first episode aired in December 1955, the throwaway melody became an instant smash, remaining number one on the Hit Parade for thirteen weeks and selling over ten million records.

CANDLE ON THE WATER

Pete's Dragon features an all-star cast headlined by Helen Reddy, Mickey Rooney, Jim Dale—and Elliott, the animated dragon. With lyrics and music by Oscar winners Al Kasha and Joel Hirschhorn, *Pete's Dragon* is rich in memorable musical moments. "Candle on the Water" is sung by Helen Reddy and, as Kasha has pointed out, "This is a step-out song. That is, Helen steps out of the action, goes up to the lighthouse, and it gives her an opportunity in the film to fully utilize her talent for singing a ballad."

"Candle on the Water" received an Academy Award nomination for Best Song.

GIVE A LITTLE WHISTLE

Jiminy Cricket is such a dominant figure in Disney's *Pinocchio* that he sings the film's two major hit songs, "When You Wish Upon a Star" and "Give a Little Whistle." His challenging task is to teach the newly-brought-to-life puppet right from wrong. Jiminy's snappy personality comes through as he musically advises Pinoke to "give a little whistle, and always let your conscience be your guide!"

BABY MINE
(From Walt Disney's "DUMBO")

Words by NED WASHINGTON
Music by FRANK CHURCHILL

THE BALLAD OF DAVY CROCKETT

Words by TOM BLACKBURN
Music by GEORGE BRUNS

VERSES

4.
Andy Jackson is our gen'ral's name,
His reg'lar soldiers we'll put to shame,
Them redskin varmints us Volunteers'll tame,
'Cause we got the guns with the sure-fire aim.
Davy — Davy Crockett,
The champion of us all!

5.
Headed back to war from the ol' home place,
But Red Stick was leadin' a merry chase,
Fightin' an' burnin' at a devil's pace
South to the swamps on the Florida Trace.
Davy — Davy Crockett,
Trackin' the redskins down!

6.
Fought single-handed through the Injun War
Till the Creeks was whipped an' peace was in store,
An' while he was handlin' this risky chore,
Made hisself a legend for evermore.
Davy — Davy Crockett,
King of the wild frontier!

7.
He give his word an' he give his hand
That his Injun friends could keep their land,
An' the rest of his life he took the stand
That justice was due every redskin band.
Davy — Davy Crockett,
Holdin' his promise dear!

8.
Home fer the winter with his family,
Happy as squirrels in the ol' gum tree,
Bein' the father he wanted to be,
Close to his boys as the pod an' the pea.
Davy — Davy Crockett,
Holdin' his young 'uns dear!

9.
But the ice went out an' the warm winds came
An' the meltin' snow showed tracks of game,
An' the flowers of Spring filled the woods with flame,
An' all of a sudden life got too tame.
Davy — Davy Crockett,
Headin' on West again!

10.
Off through the woods we're riding' along,
Makin' up yarns an' singin' a song,
He's ringy as a b'ar an' twict as strong,
An' knows he's right 'cause he ain't often wrong.
Davy — Davy Crockett,
The man who don't know fear!

11.
Lookin' fer a place where the air smells clean,
Where the trees is tall an' the grass is green,
Where the fish is fat in an untouched stream,
An' the teemin' woods is a hunter's dream.
Davy — Davy Crockett,
Lookin' fer Paradise!

12.
Now he'd lost his love an' his grief was gall,
In his heart he wanted to leave it all,
An' lose himself in the forests tall,
But he answered instead his country's call.
Davy — Davy Crockett,
Beginnin' his campaign!

13.
Needin' his help they didn't vote blind,
They put in Davy 'cause he was their kind,
Sent up to Nashville the best they could find,
A fightin' spirit an' a thinkin' mind.
Davy — Davy Crockett,
Choice of the whole frontier!

14.
The votes were counted an' he won hands down,
So they sent him off to Washin'ton town
With his best dress suit still his buckskins brown,
A livin' legend of growin' renown.
Davy — Davy Crockett,
The Canebrake Congressman!

15.
He went off to Congress an' served a spell,
Fixin' up the Gover'ment an' laws as well,
Took over Washin'ton so we heered tell
An' patched up the crack in the Liberty Bell.
Davy — Davy Crockett,
Seein' his duty clear!

16.
Him an' his jokes travelled all through the land,
An' his speeches made him friends to beat the band,
His politickin' was their favorite brand
An' everyone wanted to shake his hand.
Davy — Davy Crockett,
Helpin' his legend grow!

17.
He knew when he spoke he sounded the knell
Of his hopes for White House an' fame as well,
But he spoke out strong so hist'ry books tell
An patched up the crack in the Liberty Bell.
Davy — Davy Crockett,
Seein' his duty clear!

BEST OF FRIENDS
(From Walt Disney's "THE FOX AND THE HOUND")

Words by STAN FIDEL
Music by RICHARD JOHNSTON

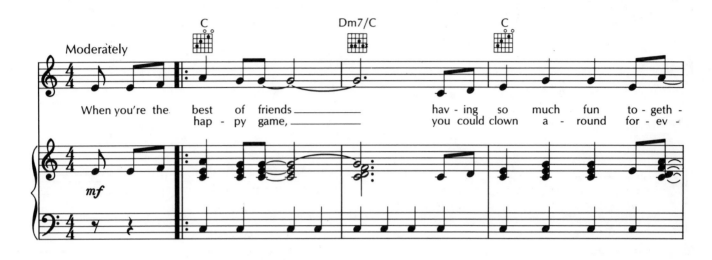

When you're the best of friends _____ hav-ing so much fun to-geth-
hap-py game, _____ you could clown a-round for-ev-

-er, you're not e-ven a-ware _____ you're such a fun-ny pair. _____
-er. Nei-ther one of you sees _____ your nat-ur'l bound-a-ries. _____

You're the best _ of friends. _ Life's a   Life's one hap-py game.

BARE NECESSITIES

Words and Music by
TERRY GILKYSON

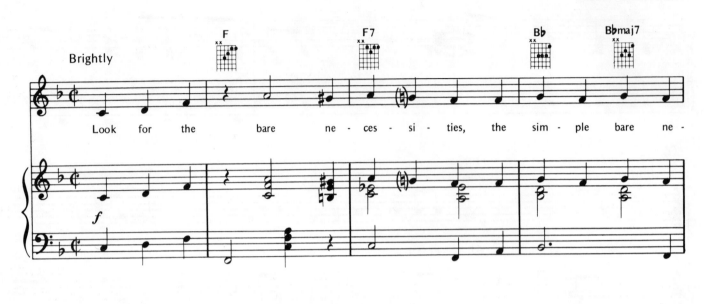

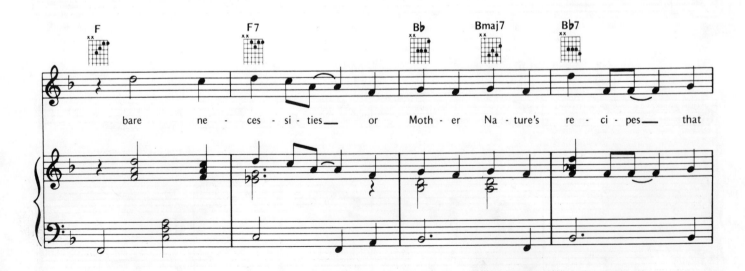

BELLA NOTTE
(From Walt Disney's "LADY AND THE TRAMP")

Words and Music by PEGGY LEE
and SONNY BURKE

BIBBIDI-BOBBIDI-BOO
(From Walt Disney's "CINDERELLA")

Words by JERRY LIVINGSTON
Music by MACK DAVID and AL HOFFMAN

CANDLE ON THE WATER

(From Walt Disney Productions' "PETE'S DRAGON")

Words and Music by AL KASHA
and JOEL HIRSCHHORN

Lyrics (first line / second line):

I'll be your can-dle on the wa-ter, My love for you will al-ways
I'll be your can-dle on the wa-ter, 'Til ev-'ry wave is warm and

burn. / bright, I know you're lost and drift-ing, But the clouds are lift-ing,
My soul is there be-side you, Let this can-dle guide you

don't give up you have some-where to turn.
soon you'll see a gold-en stream of light.

20

EV'RYBODY WANTS TO BE A CAT

(From Walt Disney's "THE ARISTOCATS")

Words by FLOYD HUDDLESTON
Music by AL RINKER

With a beat

Ev - 'ry-bod - y wants to be a cat, be-cause a cat's the on - ly cat who

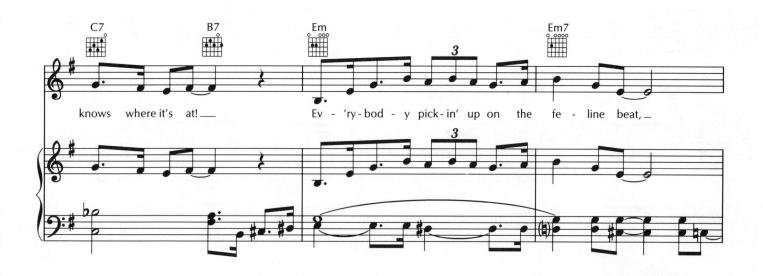

knows where it's at! ___ Ev - 'ry-bod - y pick-in' up on the fe - line beat, ___

'cause ev-'ry-thing else is ob - so - lete. Be - ware of a square ___ when he of - fers to share ___ his

CASEY JUNIOR
(From Walt Disney's "DUMBO")

Words by NED WASHINGTON
Music by FRANK CHURCHILL

Brightly

It's Cas - ey Jun - ior, com - in' down' the track___
Hear him puff - in'_____ 'round the hill___

Com - in' down the track___ with a smok - y stack.___
Cas - ey's here to thrill___ ev - 'ry Jack and Jill.___

Ev - 'ry time his fun - ny lit - tle

CHIM CHIM CHER-EE

(From Walt Disney's "MARY POPPINS")

Words and Music by
RICHARD M. SHERMAN
and ROBERT B. SHERMAN

CRUELLA DE VILLE

(From Walt Disney's "ONE HUNDRED AND ONE DALMATIONS")

Words and Music by
MEL LEVEN

A Dream Is A Wish Your Heart Makes

(From Walt Disney's "CINDERELLA")

Words and Music by MACK DAVID,
AL HOFFMAN and JERRY LIVINGSTON

FOLLOWING THE LEADER
(From Walt Disney's "PETER PAN")

Words by TED SEARS and WINSTON HIBLER
Music by OLIVER WALLACE

Gaily

Fol - low-ing the lead - er, the lead - er, the lead - er, we're

fol - low-ing the lead - er wher-ev - er he may go. _____ We

won't be home till morn - ing, till morn - ing, till morn - ing, We

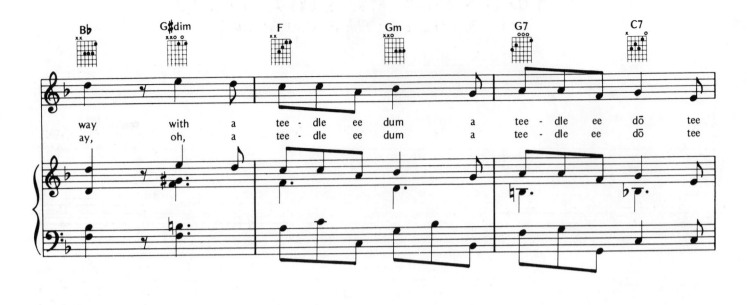

I WAN'NA BE LIKE YOU
(From Walt Disney's "THE JUNGLE BOOK")

Words and Music by RICHARD M. SHERMAN
and ROBERT B. SHERMAN

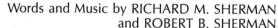

GIVE A LITTLE WHISTLE
(From "PINOCCHIO")

Words by NED WASHINGTON
Music by LEIGH HARLINE

When you get in trou - ble and you don't know right from wrong;
When you meet temp - ta - tion, and the urge is ver - y strong;
Give a lit - tle

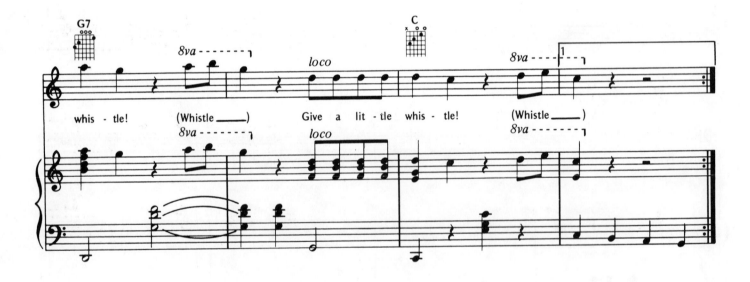

whis - tle! (Whistle ___) Give a lit - tle whis - tle! (Whistle ___)

___) Not just a lit - tle squeak; Puck - er up and

HE'S A TRAMP
(From Walt Disney's "LADY AND THE TRAMP")

Words and Music by PEGGY LEE
and SONNY BURKE

he'll show up; He gives you plen-ty of trou-ble. I guess he's just a

no 'count pup,— But I wish that he were dou-ble. He's a tramp, he's a

rov-er And there's noth-ing more to say. If he's a tramp, he's a

good one And I wish that I could trav-el his way.

8va lower

HEIGH-HO
(THE DWARFS' MARCHING SONG from "SNOW WHITE AND THE SEVEN DWARFS")

Words by LARRY MOREY
Music by FRANK CHURCHILL

HI-DIDDLE-DEE-DEE

(An Actor's Life For Me)
(From Walt Disney's "PINOCCHIO")

Words by NED WASHINGTON
Music by LEIGH HARLINE

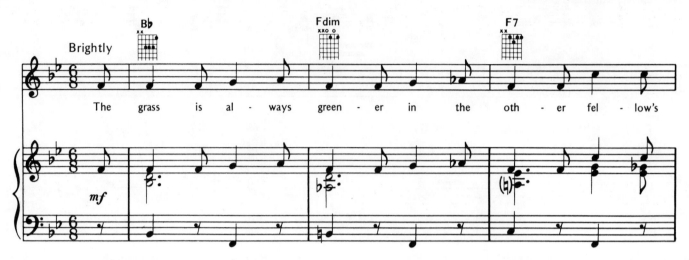

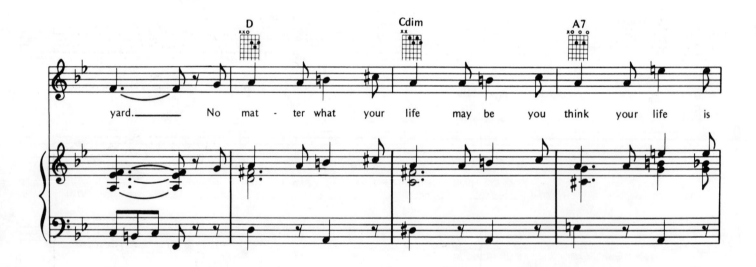

I'VE GOT NO STRINGS
(From "PINOCCHIO")

Words by NED WASHINGTON
Music by LEIGH HARLINE

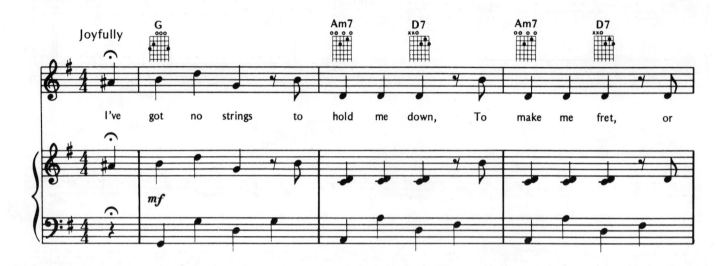

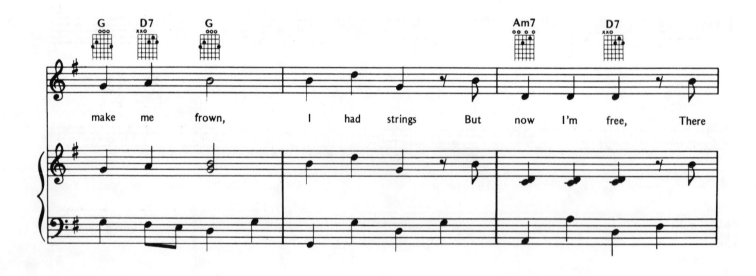

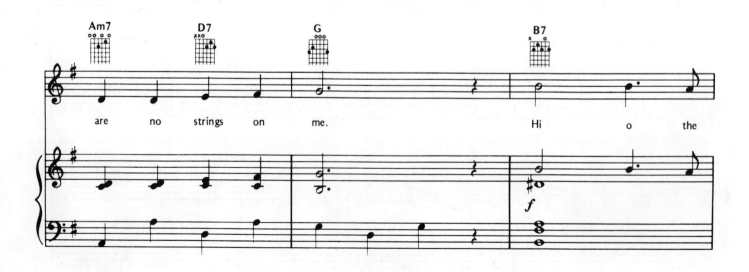

51

I WONDER

(From Walt Disney's "SLEEPING BEAUTY")

Words by WINSTON HIBLER and TED SEARS
Music by GEORGE BRUNS (Adapted From Tschaikowsky Theme)

IT'S A SMALL WORLD

(Theme from The Disneyland and Walt Disney World Attraction, "IT'S A SMALL WORLD")

Words and Music by RICHARD M. SHERMAN
AND ROBERT B. SHERMAN

March Tempo

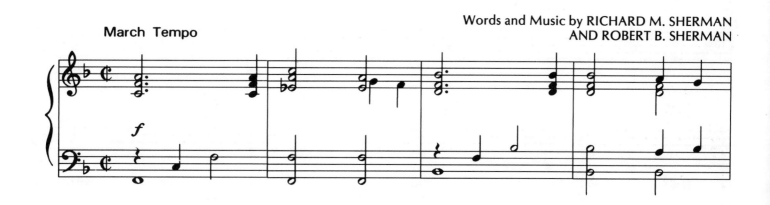

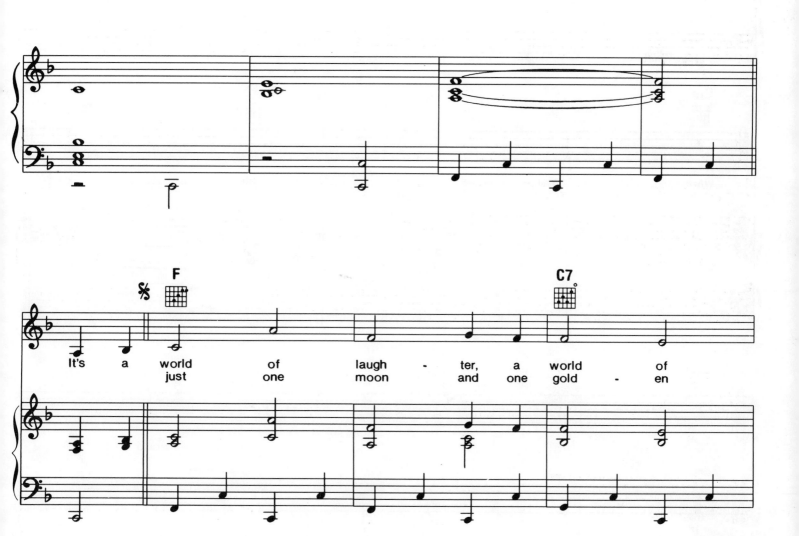

It's a world of laugh-ter, a world of
just one moon and one gold-en

LAVENDER BLUE
(Dilly Dilly)

Words by LARRY MOREY
Music by ELIOT DANIEL

Great grand-fa-ther met great grand-moth-er when she was a shy young Miss, And

great grand-fa-ther won great grand-moth-er with words more or less like this.

Lav-en-der blue dil-ly, dil-ly, lav-en-der green;

SALUDOS AMIGOS
(From Walt Disney's "THE THREE CABALLEROS")

Words by NED WASHINGTON
Music by CHARLES WOLCOTT

There's a phrase now-a-days folks are us - ing, _____ It's an old one _____ that's al - ways new; _____ If you run in - to friends in your cruis - ing, _____ This friend - ly

63

LITTLE APRIL SHOWER
(From Walt Disney's "BAMBI")

Words by LARRY MOREY
Music by FRANK CHURCHILL

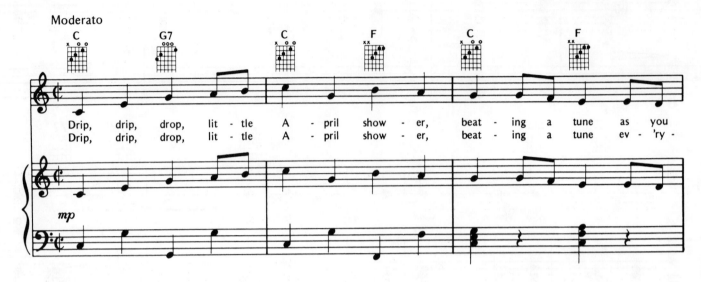

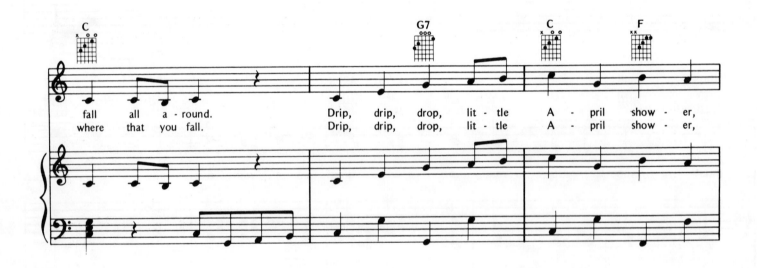

LOVE IS A SONG
(From Walt Disney's "BAMBI")

Words by LARRY MOREY
Music by FRANK CHURCHILL

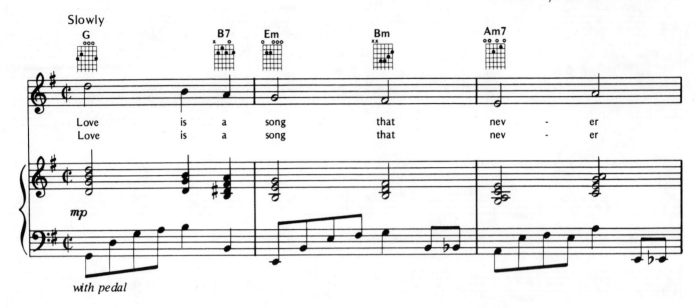

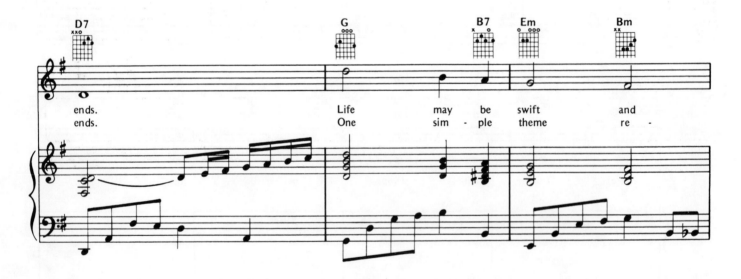

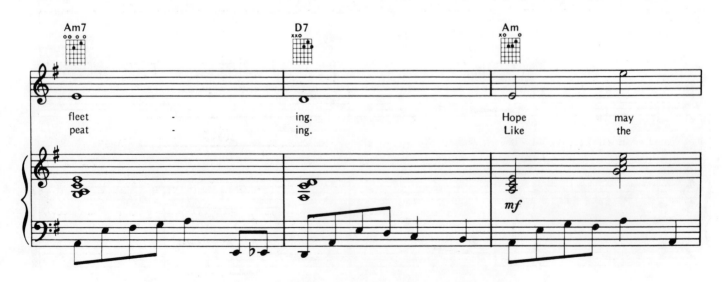

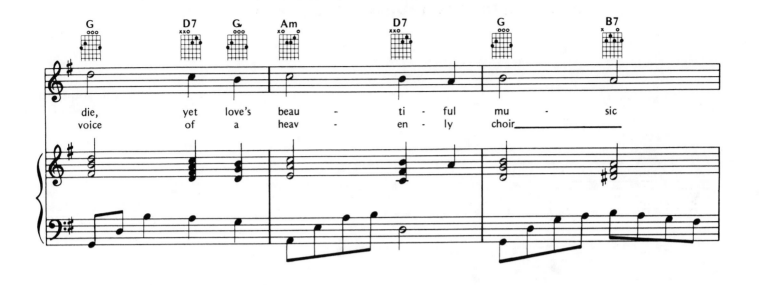

die, yet love's beau - ti - ful mu - sic
voice of a heav - en - ly choir_____

comes each day like the dawn._____
love's sweet

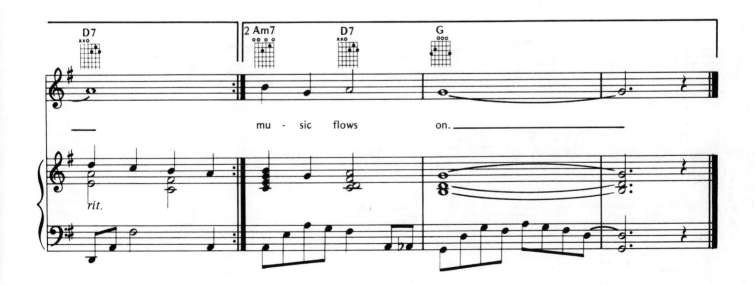

____ mu - sic flows on._____

MICKEY MOUSE ALMA MATER

(From Walt Disney's TV Series "MICKEY MOUSE CLUB")

Words and Music by
JIMMIE DODD

MICKEY MOUSE CLUB MARCH

Words and Music by
JIMMIE DODD

ONCE UPON A DREAM

(From Walt Disney's "SLEEPING BEAUTY")

Words and Music by SAMMY FAIN
and JACK LAWRENCE

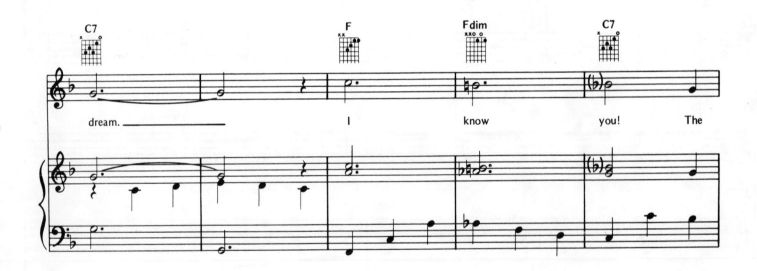

ONE SONG
(From Walt Disney's "SNOW WHITE AND THE SEVEN DWARFS")

Words by LARRY MOREY
Music by FRANK CHURCHILL

OO-DE-LALLY
(From Walt Disney's "ROBIN HOOD")

Words and Music by
ROGER MILLER

Moderately

Rob- in Hood and Lit- tle John walk- in' thru the for- est, Laugh- in' back and forth at what the
Rob- in Hood and Lit- tle John run- nin' thru the for- est, Jump- in' fen- ces dodg- in' trees and

mf

oth- er 'un has to say. _____ Re- min- isc- in' this 'n that 'n
try- in' to get a- way. _____ Con- tem- pla- tin' noth- in' but es-

hav- in' such a good time.
cape and fin- 'ly makin' it. } Oo- de- lal- ly, Hoo- de- lal- ly, Gol- ly what a day! _____

THE SECOND STAR TO THE RIGHT
(From Walt Disney's "PETER PAN")

Words by SAMMY CAHN
Music by SAMMY FAIN

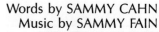

Slowly, with expression

The sec - ond star to the right shines in the night for
The sec - ond star to the right shines with a light that's

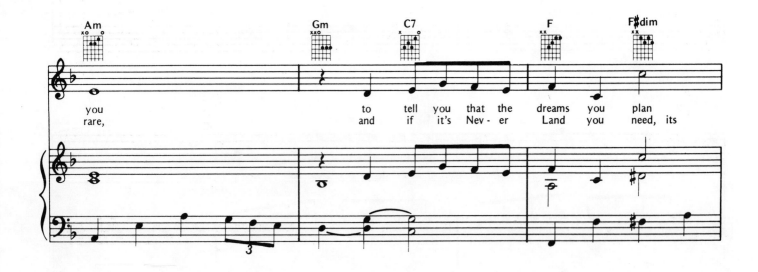

you rare,
and if it's Nev - er Land you to tell you that the dreams you plan need, its

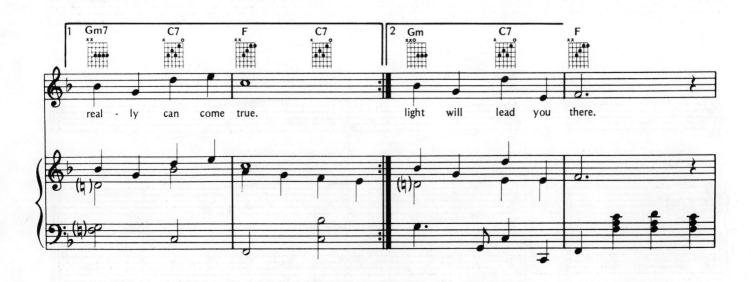

real - ly can come true.
light will lead you there.

THE SIAMESE CAT SONG

Words and Music by PEGGY LEE
and SONNY BURKE

We are Si - am-ese with ver - y dain -ty claws.

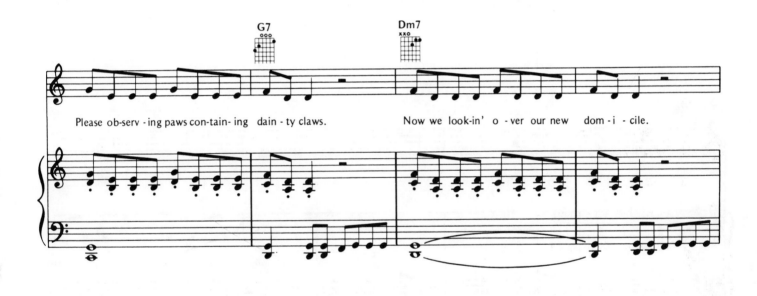

Please ob-serv -ing paws con-tain- ing dain - ty claws.

Now we look-in' o -ver our new dom -i - cile.

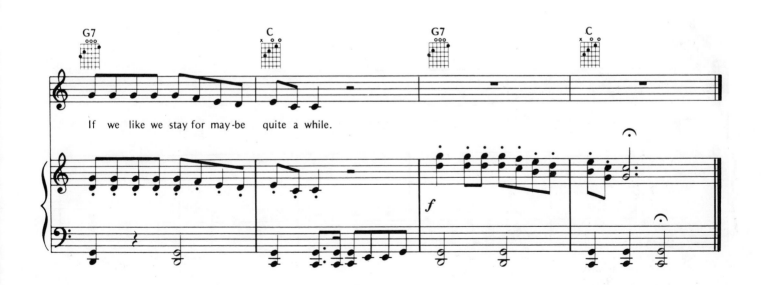

If we like we stay for may -be quite a while.

SO THIS IS LOVE
(From Walt Disney's "CINDERELLA")

Words by MACK DAVID,
AL HOFFMAN and JERRY LIVINGSTON

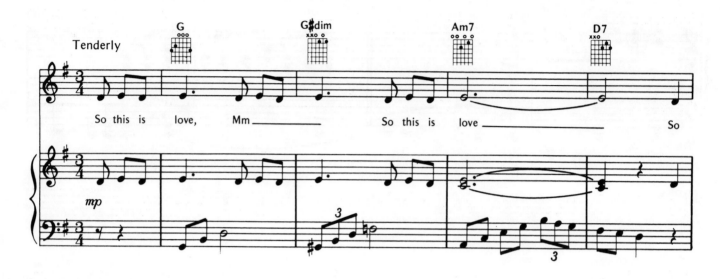

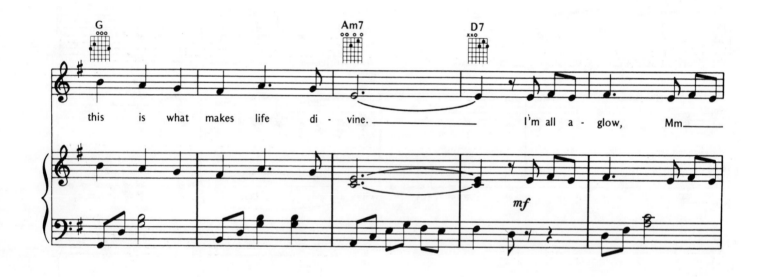

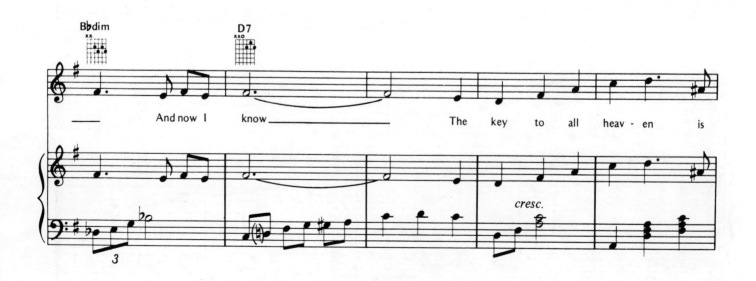

SOME DAY MY PRINCE WILL COME
(From Walt Disney's "SNOW WHITE AND THE SEVEN DWARFS")

Words by LARRY MOREY
Music by FRANK CHURCHILL

SOMEONE'S WAITING FOR YOU

(From Walt Disney's "THE RESCUERS")

Words by CAROL CONNORS and AYN ROBBINS
Music by SAMMY FAIN

Slowly

Ev-'ry child has man-y wish-es that they wish when they're a-

lone. Faith can work just like mag-ic; noth-ing chang-es when you're

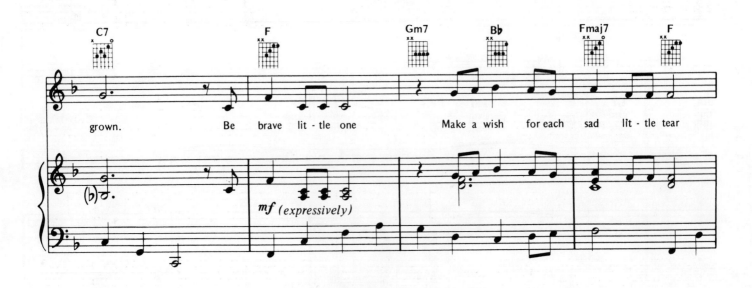

grown. Be brave lit-tle one Make a wish for each sad lit-tle tear

A SPOONFUL OF SUGAR

Words and Music by RICHARD M. SHERMAN
and ROBERT B. SHERMAN

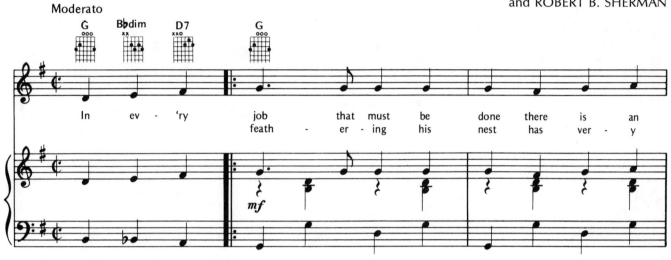

In ev - 'ry job that must be done there is an
feath - er - ing his nest has ver - y

el - e - ment of fun; You find the fun and
lit - tle time to rest While gath - er - ing his

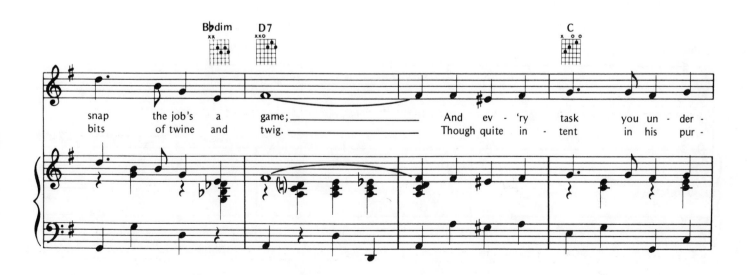

snap the job's a game;_____ And ev - 'ry task you un - der-
bits of twine and twig._____ Though quite in - tent in his pur-

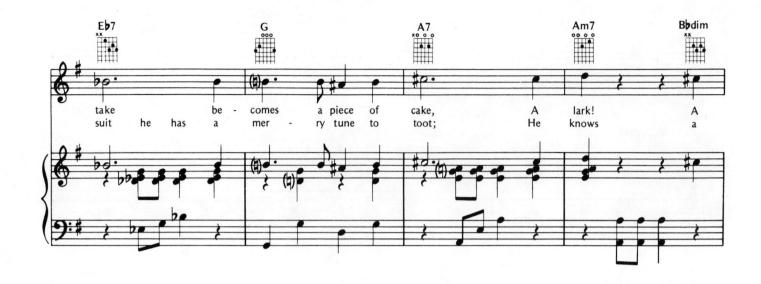

take — be - comes a piece of cake, A lark! A
suit he has a mer - ry tune to toot; He knows a

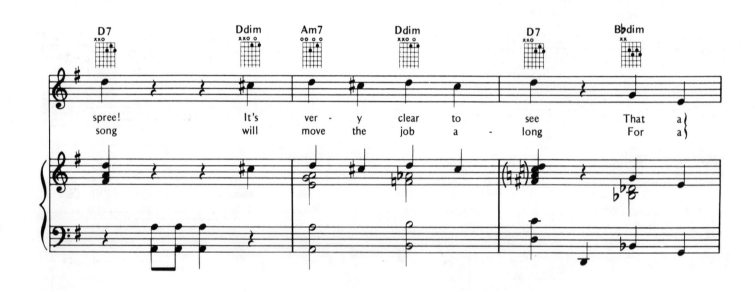

spree! It's ver - y clear to see That a
song will move the job a - long For a

spoon - ful of su - gar helps the med - i - cine go

SUPERCALIFRAGILISTICEXPIALIDOCIOUS

(From Walt Disney's "MARY POPPINS")

Words and Music by RICHARD M. SHERMAN
and ROBERT B. SHERMAN

MARY POPPINS
Sup - er - cal - i - frag - il - is - tic - ex - pi - al - i - do - cious!

E - ven though the sound of it is some - thing quite a - tro - cious,

If you say it loud e - nough, you'll al - ways sound pre - co - cious.

THEME FROM ZORRO

Words by NORMAN FOSTER
Music by GEORGE BRUNS

8va - - - - - -

WHEN YOU WISH UPON A STAR
(From Walt Disney's "PINOCCHIO")

Words by NED WASHINGTON
Music by LEIGH HARLINE

WHEN I SEE AN ELEPHANT FLY

(From "DUMBO")

Words by NED WASHINGTON
Music by OLIVER WALLACE

WHISTLE WHILE YOU WORK

(From Walt Disney's "SNOW WHITE AND THE SEVEN DWARFS")

Words by LARRY MOREY
Music by FRANK CHURCHILL

WHO'S AFRAID OF THE BIG BAD WOLF?

(From "THE THREE LITTLE PIGS")

Words and Music by FRANK CHURCHILL
Additional Lyric by ANN RONELL

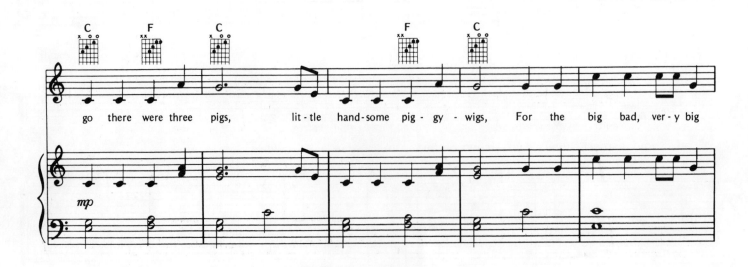

WITH A SMILE AND A SONG

(From Walt Disney's "SNOW WHITE AND THE SEVEN DWARFS")

Words by LARRY MOREY
Music by FRANK CHURCHILL

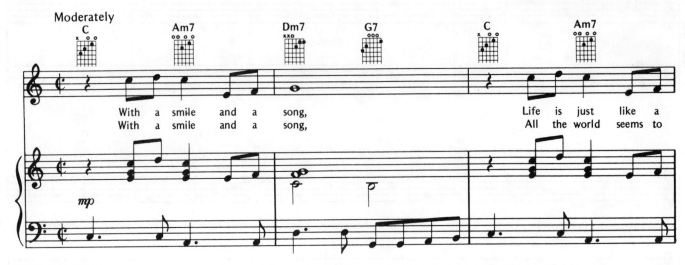

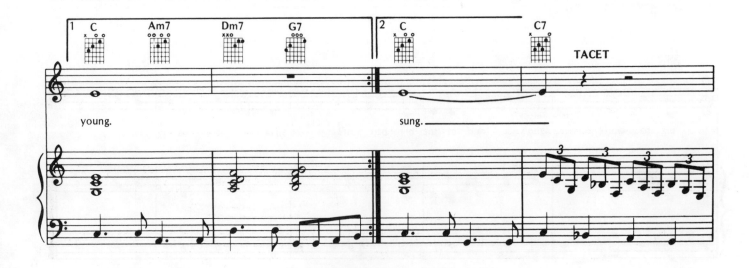

THE WORK SONG

Words and Music by MACK DAVID,
AL HOFFMAN and JERRY LIVINGSTON

YO, HO
(A PIRATE'S LIFE FOR ME)

Words by XAVIER ATENCIO
Music by GEORGE BRUNS

YOU CAN FLY! YOU CAN FLY! YOU CAN FLY!

Moderately

Words by SAMMY CAHN
Music by SAMMY FAIN

Think of the pres-ents you've brought
When there's a smile in your heart

An - y mer-ry lit-tle thought
There's no bet-ter time to start

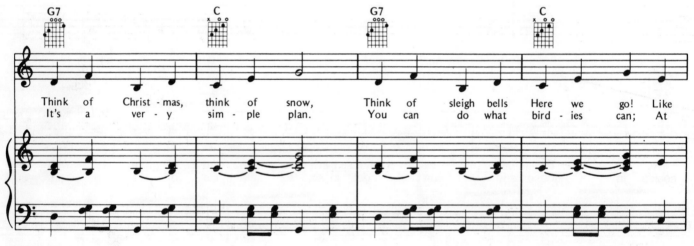

Think of Christ-mas, think of snow,
It's a ver - y sim - ple plan.

Think of sleigh bells Here we go! Like
You can do what bird - ies can; At

rein - deer in the sky
least it's worth a try

You can fly! You can

To Coda

ZIP-A-DEE-DOO-DAH
(From Walt Disney's "SONG OF THE SOUTH")

Words by RAY GILBERT
Music by ALLIE WRUBEL

WINNIE THE POOH

Words and Music by RICHARD M. SHERMAN
and ROBERT B. SHERMAN

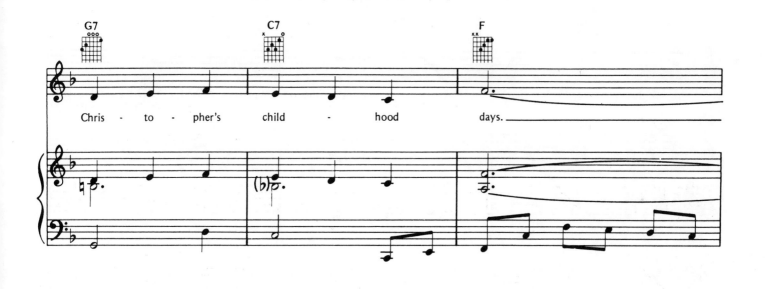

Chris - to - pher's child - hood days. _____

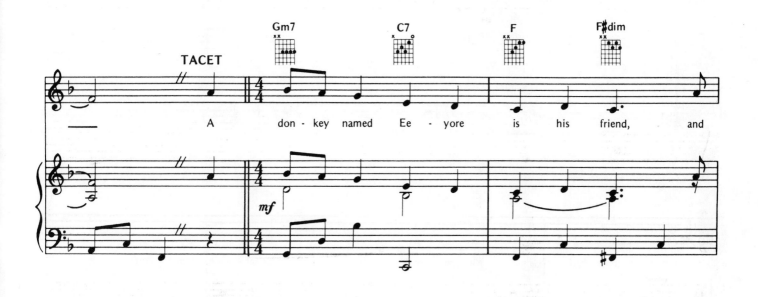

TACET

_____ A don - key named Ee - yore is his friend, and

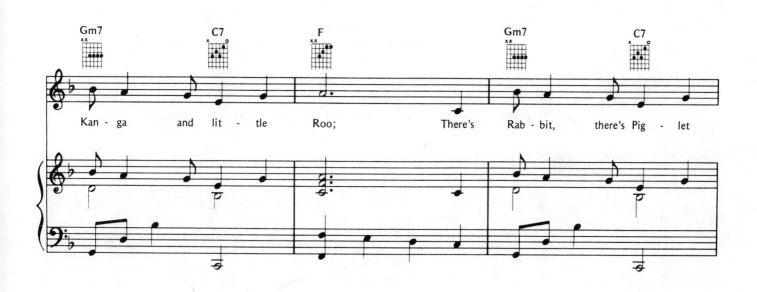

Kan - ga and lit - tle Roo; There's Rab - bit, there's Pig - let